Proudly presented to:

IN CELEBRATION OF YOUR LOST TOOTH AND BEAUTIFUL SMILE!

Love Always,

Date:

For Chris, Tanner, and Faren,
whose smiles have inspired this book and my life.
–L.M.

For Jack, Anna & Charlie with all my love, Mom
–C.B.

Printed in the USA
Published by Heartsong Press ™
Copyright © 2020 by Lindsey Montes de Oca

Written by
LINDSEY MONTES DE OCA

Illustrated by
CHRISTY BERGERSON

Hip hip hooray! You've lost a tooth!
Now I must tell you an important truth.

For now, have fun with that gap in your smile
but I'll be moving in after awhile.

It's me! Your little forever tooth.
If you want, you can name me... Sam, Buddy or Ruth?

I'll be with you
every season as you grow,
enjoying the sunshine,
the rain, and the snow.

I'll do my best to be helpful to you
because you'll need my help to talk and to chew.

I will be with you wherever you roam,
on your car rides around town and back to your home.

We'll have fun singing and giving book reports.
Remember to protect me when you're playing sports!

Basketball,
football,
ballet
or chess,

I'm a part of you,
and we try our best.

We'll have picnics in the park and
ride the swings up so high.

And I'll be your travel buddy eating plane snacks in the sky.

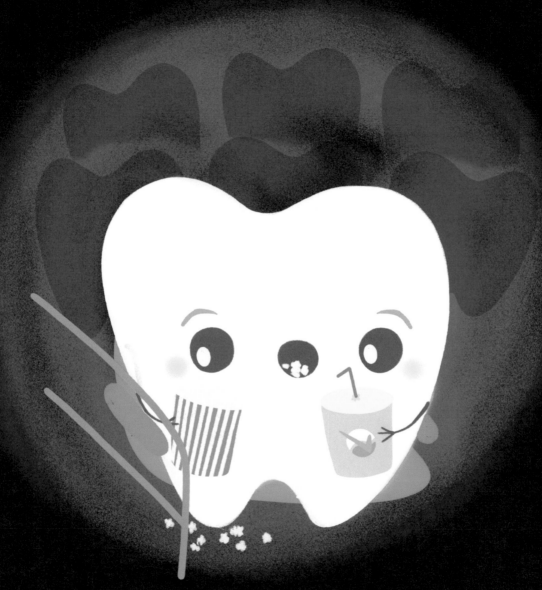

I'll watch movies with you while
enjoying theater treats,

and we'll munch on concession stand
foods while in stadium seats.

For every breakfast,
lunch, dinner, and snack,
I'm here to help you.
I've got your back.

Sitting at all the family
meals you'll share,
I'm happy to report that
I'll be right there.

Can I tell you how excited I am for all of the ways
that I'll be with you on holidays?

After your pumpkin is full of Trick or Treat candy,
I will come in very handy.

We'll eat filled Easter eggs, valentines
and festive sweets galore!

And sharing the feast on Thanksgiving?
That's what I'm here for!

Every year I'll be there as you make
special wishes on your birthday cake,

and smiling by your side for all
those big life steps you will take.

I look forward to all
of my adventures with you.
Please take care of me
no matter what you do.

Take me to
the dentist and
brush each day
and night,

so I can stay
strong and
pearly white.

I can't wait to meet you! I'm on my way!
Soon we'll be together everyday.

Although I'm just a tiny part of you,
I'm so proud to be a part of all the amazing things you'll do.

the
end.